Karen's Kittens

**Look for these
and other books about Karen
in the
Baby-sitters Little Sister series:**

Little Sister

Karen's Kittens
Ann M. Martin

Illustrations by Susan Tang

A
LITTLE APPLE
PAPERBACK

SCHOLASTIC INC.
New York Toronto London Auckland Sydney

No part of this publication may be reproduced in whole or in part, or stored in a retrieval system, or transmitted in any form or by any means, electronic, mechanical, photocopying, recording, or otherwise, without written permission of the publisher. For information regarding permission, write to Scholastic Inc., 730 Broadway, New York, NY 10003.

ISBN 0-590-45645-8

12 11 10   7/9

Printed in the U.S.A.   40

First Scholastic printing, July 1992

The author gratefully acknowledges
Stephanie Calmenson
for her help
with this book.

Karen's Kittens

Rainy Day

Plink! Plunk! Plink! Plunk!

Raindrops were falling on the lid of the garbage can out in the yard. The noise was making me crabby. I am usually not a crabby person. I am usually a gigundoly happy person.

My name is Karen Brewer. I am seven years old. I have blonde hair, blue eyes, and a bunch of freckles. Oh, yes, I wear glasses, too.

My brother, Andrew, is four going on five. He looks a lot like me, but he does not have so many freckles and he does not need glasses.

I had been listening to the raindrops falling — *plink! plunk! plink! plunk!* — ever since I got home from school. That was ages ago.

Andrew had been home even longer. That is because he is not in real school yet. He is in preschool, which is only half a day.

And poor Emily Junior had been home all day long. Emily Junior does not go to school. That is because she is a rat — my pet rat. Hmmm. Maybe someday she will follow me to school like Mary's little lamb. That would be an adventure. And I love adventures.

I have been training Emily Junior to be a circus rat. I know she is going to be a great star someday. She just needs a little more practice.

"Jump, Emily, jump!" I said.

"You keep telling her to jump, but all she does is run in circles," said Andrew.

"Maybe in rat language jump means run. And run means jump," I said.

Andrew rolled his eyes.

"Watch this," I said. "Run, Emily, run!"

Emily Junior laid down and went to sleep. I guess in rat language run means sleep.

"Let's see if Rocky and Midgie want to play," said Andrew.

Midgie is Seth's dog. (Seth is our stepfather.) Rocky is his cat.

"Okay," I said. "We can dress them in secret disguises. Then we can see if Seth recognizes them when he comes home."

Andrew and I went downstairs to find Midgie and Rocky. We found them all right. They were curled up together under the kitchen table. They were fast asleep.

"Seth said we should not bother them when they are sleeping," I reminded Andrew.

Plink! Plunk! Plink! Plunk!

"I know what. I will call Nancy. We can

have a rainy day tea party," I said. Nancy Dawes is one of my two best friends. Hannie Papadakis is my other best friend. We call ourselves the Three Musketeers.

I was counting on Nancy to save the day. I dialed her number. The phone rang once. It rang twice. It rang three times. Boo. No one was home.

Andrew and I had already played about a million games of Go Fish. We were just going to have to play a million and one. I took the cards out of the box again.

"Bor-ing!" said Andrew.

"Oh, well," I said. "Soon we will be at the big house. We are never bored there. At the big house something interesting is always going on."

Pets Everywhere

Not many people have two houses. But Andrew and I do. We have the little house and the big house. I will tell you why, starting from the very beginning.

A long time ago Mommy and Daddy got married. While they were married, they had Andrew and me. Then things started to change. Mommy and Daddy loved Andrew and me a lot. But they decided they did not love each other anymore. At least not enough to stay married. So they got a divorce.

Mommy and Andrew and I moved out of the big house in Stoneybrook, Connecticut. That is the house Daddy grew up in. We moved into a little house not too far away. After a while, Mommy met a nice man named Seth and they got married. That is how Seth got to be our stepfather. And that is how Midgie, Seth's dog, and Rocky, Seth's cat, came to live with us.

Meanwhile, back at the big house, Daddy got married again, too. He married a nice woman named Elizabeth. And she moved in with her four children. Now they are my stepbrothers and stepsister. They are: Charlie and Sam, who are in high school; David Michael, who is seven, like me, only he likes to brag that he is a few months older than I am; and Kristy, who is thirteen. Kristy happens to be one of my most favorite people in the whole world. She reads to me and talks to me and plays with me. And she is a great baby-sitter, too.

That is not all. I have an adopted sister named Emily Michelle. Daddy and Elizabeth adopted her from a faraway country called Vietnam. Emily Michelle is two and a half years old. (I named my rat, Emily Junior, after her.)

The last person I will tell you about is Nannie. Nannie is Elizabeth's mother. That makes her my stepgrandmother. She takes care of Emily Michelle when Daddy and Elizabeth are at work and the rest of us are at school.

Now I can tell you about the pets at the big house. There is Shannon, David Michael's great, big Bernese mountain dog puppy. There is Boo-Boo, Daddy's fat, mean old cat. There is Crystal Light the Second, my goldfish. And there is Goldfishie, Andrew's you-know-what.

Andrew and I live at the little house most of the time. But every other weekend and on some vacations and holidays, we live at the big house.

To make things easier, Andrew and I

have two of almost everything. That is why I call us Karen Two-Two and Andrew Two-Two. (I thought up those names after my teacher, Ms. Colman, read a book to our class. It was called *Jacob Two-Two Meets the Hooded Fang*.)

I have two bicycles, one at each house. I have two sets of clothes, toys, and books. I have my two best friends: Nancy lives next door to the little house and Hannie lives across the street and one house over from the big house. I have two stuffed cats. Goosie lives at the little house. Moosie lives at the big house. And I have two pieces of my special blanket, Tickly. (I kept leaving Tickly at one house or the other. Finally I had to rip Tickly in half. But I do not think it hurt much.)

Guess what I did the other day. I counted all the people and all the pets at my two houses. (I am very good at math.) Here is what I got: four people and three pets at the little house, and eight people (not counting me and Andrew because we only live there sometimes) and four pets at the big house. That makes twelve people and seven pets altogether. I have people and pets everywhere!

I think there are enough people. But sometimes I wish I had more pets. A rat and a goldfish are nice to have. But I would like to have a cat or a kitten of my own, too. Or maybe *two* cats or kittens! One for each house. After all, I am Karen Two-Two.

"I'm Bored"

"See you later, alligators!" called Mommy as we raced up the driveway of Daddy's house.

I really did feel like an alligator sloshing through the mud in my green rainboots and slicker.

The door opened before we even had a chance to knock. Our whole big-house family was waiting to greet us!

"Hi, kids," said Daddy. He usually gives us each a big hug. But we were dripping wet. Daddy helped Andrew take off his slicker.

"Come on, Karen," said Kristy. "I'll help you get your boots off."

"Yo, Professor, I think you need wind-shield wipers on your glasses!" said David Michael. (My glasses are the reason he calls me "Professor.")

"Very funny," I said. But maybe wind-shield wipers were not such a bad idea. I just had to figure out a way to attach them. They would look cool!

"Why don't you kids go to your rooms and unpack," said Elizabeth. "Dinner will be ready soon."

I love my room at the big house. I said hello to Moosie and to Tickly. Then I put the book I wanted to read with Kristy on my night table. It was called *Churchkitten Stories* by Margot Austin. I figured if I could not have kittens at least I could read about them.

"Let's go, Andrew!" I called when I finished unpacking. I hurried back downstairs. There was lots of noise coming from the kitchen. I did not want anything fun to happen without me.

As soon as Andrew and I got there, Nannie brought out a big plate of hamburgers and rolls and lots of gloppy stuff to put on them. Yum!

There was a plate of tomatoes in front of Emily Michelle.

" 'Matoes, 'matoes," sang Emily Michelle. She stuck her foot up on the table and started wiggling her toes.

"I bet I never did anything silly like that when I was little," I said.

"When was that?" said Sam. "Last week?"

Sam is a big tease. I decided to act very grown-up and ignore him.

"Please pass the ketchup," I said in my most grown-up voice.

After we ate and cleaned up, I waited for something interesting to happen. Something interesting always happens at the big house. Well, almost always.

But Daddy and Elizabeth went to their room early to read. Nannie went out with a friend. Sam and Charlie went to a movie. David Michael disappeared into his room and put up a sign that said, "Do not disturb — or else." Emily Michelle was asleep. Even Shannon and Boo-Boo were pooped out.

"Hey, what is this?" I said to Andrew.

Andrew shrugged. "Want to play Go Fish?" he said.

"No way!" I replied. I ran upstairs to find Kristy. She was in her room combing her hair.

"I'm bored," I announced.

"Then find something to do," said Kristy.

"I can't," I said. "I want something fun to *happen*."

"I'm sorry I can't help you. I have a babysitting job," said Kristy. And she hurried downstairs.

"No, no, no, no, no!" I said to myself. But I got out the cards anyway and played six more games of Go Fish with Andrew.

I was so bored by the time I went to bed, that sleeping sounded like fun. Whoopee.

The Disappearing Tail

I woke up Saturday morning trying to remember what had happened the night before. Why couldn't I remember? Then I figured it out. I could not remember what happened because *nothing* happened.

"Good morning, Moosie," I said. "I hope your life is more exciting than mine these days."

I went to the playroom to check on Crystal Light. She was swimming around in the bowl. Then I remembered what I did last night. I played six games of Go Fish with Andrew.

Well, the sun was shining in my window and something was bound to happen today. After all, I was at the big house!

Nothing happened at breakfast. Except Emily Michelle spilled her bowl of Fruity-O's on the floor. And Kristy got three phone calls in a row.

"I'm going to play outside!" I called to anyone who was interested.

I looked over at Hannie's house. I knew it was empty, though. Hannie had gone away with her family for the weekend.

I looked at my other friend, Melody's, house. But I knew I would not see her either because she had gone to a ballet class.

Somebody sighed loudly. It was me. Life was gigundoly boring.

Since nothing was happening in front of the house, I checked out the backyard. I was just in time, too. As soon as I got there,

I saw a furry, gray tail disappear inside Daddy's toolshed.

What was the shed doing open? I knew that Daddy was inside the house and he always makes sure the door of the shed is closed when he's not there.

And whose furry, gray tail was it?

In case you did not know it, I happen to be a first class detective. I even had a detective agency once and solved a lot of mysteries. I would solve this mystery, too. Oh boy! This was exciting. Something was really and truly happening!

I ran to the toolshed to investigate.

"Aha!" I said. The bottom of the sliding metal doors was all rusty. They were stuck open. There was just enough space for a gray, furry-tailed thing to slip through.

I looked inside the shed. It was dark because the windows were dirty. I waited for my eyes to get used to the darkness. Hmm. Instead of windshield wipers, maybe I should attach flashlights to my glasses.

That would be a good thing for a detective to do.

Uh-oh. Something was moving in the back of the shed. It was a fat, gray tiger cat! She was making herself comfortable on a pile of old rags.

I pushed the doors open a little bit more and squeezed inside the shed. I inched closer on my tippy toes. I was trying not to scare the cat.

"A-rowwwl!" she growled.

Who was scared now? Me! I raced out of that shed.

"Dadd-eee!" I called.

Growly

"Come on, Daddy! Hurry!" I cried.

"I'm right behind you, Karen," said Daddy.

He looked pretty funny. He was wearing bright red fish-shaped oven mitts. They covered his hands and went all the way up to his elbows. That is so he would not get scratched if he tried to pick up the cat.

I slipped between the doors of the shed.

Daddy could not fit through the opening though. He had to push the doors wider apart. The sun came pouring in and I got a good look at the cat. Boy, was she fat!

Daddy took a few steps closer to her.

"A-rowwl! A-rowwl! A-rowwl!" she growled. But she did not move.

The cat looked at Daddy. Daddy looked at the cat.

"She is going to have kittens, Karen," said Daddy. "And probably pretty soon."

"Neat!" I said. "We can help her."

"We can help her best by leaving her alone. She will know what to do," said Daddy. "And we can let her raise her family here in the shed. But for now, we better not touch her."

"Not touch her?" I repeated. "Can I at least bring her some food and water?"

Daddy said that would be all right. I hurried into the kitchen. I filled a bowl with water. Then I put some of Boo-Boo's cat food on a plate. I did not bother asking Boo-Boo first. Since he was such a mean old cat, he probably would not want to share.

I ran back to the toolshed. On the way, I tripped over a rock and spilled everything. Boo. I had to pick up all the food, then fill the bowl with water again.

I hoped the cat would not have her kittens before I got back to the shed.

She didn't. I was starting to feel lucky. Saturday had started out boring. But it was not boring anymore. And I had wanted a cat or a kitten. Now I was going to have both!

I hope the kittens will be born tonight, I thought. I will get to see them before I have to go back to the little house tomorrow afternoon.

Let's see. I needed a name for the cat. What could it be? I tapped my foot on the ground while I thought. The cat did not like that.

"A-rowwwl!" she growled.

I jumped back.

"Naming you is easy," I said. "I am going to call you Growly."

Kittens!

Hundreds of cats, thousands of cats, millions and billions and trillions of cats!

It was Sunday morning. I had been dreaming of a book I read in school called *Millions of Cats*. That is how many cats I wanted to find when I went out to the toolshed. Well, maybe not that many. Especially if they growled like Growly.

My big-house family was awake. Everyone wanted to see if Growly had had her kittens yet. We marched out to the toolshed together. I was the leader.

Well, there weren't a million. Or a thousand. Or even a hundred. But there were kittens all right. Five tiny ones nursing away at Growly.

"Ooh," said Elizabeth.

"Aw," said Daddy.

"They are so pudgy," said Kristy.

"They are so little," said Andrew.

"They are so . . . ugly," I said. I made a face. "I thought they would be cute and cuddly like the kittens on TV commercials. You know, the ones for kitten chow."

"Don't worry, Karen," said Elizabeth. "Kittens grow fast. You will see changes in them every day."

"I hope so," I said. These things were squirmy. Their eyes were closed. They looked a little like rats. But not cute rats like Emily Junior.

I took a step closer to see if I could find anything cute about them.

"Don't touch them yet," warned Kristy.

"I won't," I promised. I stared and stared. And you know what? I decided they were cute after all — even if they were not funny and fluffy like the TV kittens. I decided they were sweet.

"I changed my mind!" I announced. "I think they are cute after all. So, Daddy, can we keep Growly and her kittens?"

"I'm sorry, honey," said Daddy. "We have way too many pets in our house already."

"Oh, please, puh-lease!" I cried. "After all, they were born here, so they belong here."

"They really are cute and sweet," said Kristy. "Can't we keep just a couple?"

"No, we cannot," said Daddy.

"I want a kitten!" said Andrew.

"Kitty!" said Emily Michelle.

"The answer is no and that is final," said Daddy. "But I will tell you what. We can let Growly stay here until the kittens are grown up enough to leave her. By then, I hope we will have figured out what to do with them."

"When will that be?" I asked.

"Kittens can usually leave their mother in about eight weeks," said Elizabeth.

Eight weeks! That was a long time. Two months. I would get to watch them grow.

I looked at Growly with her five little kittens all in a row. She looked tired. But I think she looked proud, too.

"Congratulations, Growly," I whispered. "You did a good job."

Birth Announcements

"Time for breakfast, everyone," said Nannie.

"Good idea," said Sam. "Watching these kittens eat is making me hungry."

Andrew and I stayed behind after everyone else left. Who cared about eating when you could watch newborn kittens?

"Andrew, listen!" I whispered.

The kittens were making little squeaking noises. They hardly sounded like cats at all.

"Growly's a good mommy," said Andrew.

"She sure is," I said. The kittens were finished eating. They were crawling all over Growly. She was very patient with them.

Guess what. The kittens could not see yet. Their eyes had not opened. They were stepping on each other's tails and paws and ears and eyes. They looked so funny!

Now I will tell you what the kittens looked like.

Two were mostly gray. But one had a white tip on his tail, and the other had two white paws.

One kitten was all black. And the other two were gray tiger-striped like Growly. I could tell them apart because one had a black diamond on her forehead.

We learned in school that kittens' colors change as they get older. (For a while, I had wondered if Goosie's and Moosie's colors would change. But they never did.)

"Whoa! Look at that," I said. The black kitten had tumbled off Growly's back. I wondered if I should make sure he was all right. But Growly was taking care of him. She was licking him. I heard him squeak so I knew he was okay.

"Let's go see if there is any breakfast left," I said to my brother.

"I hope there is," said Andrew. "I'm hungry."

On the way back to the house, I had an idea. It was not just any old idea. It was a great idea!

When babies are born, parents usually send out birth announcements. But I could see that Growly was way too busy to do it herself. So I would do it for her.

While I ate breakfast, I thought about what the announcements should say. By the time I was finished, I had planned everything.

I went to my room and got busy. I picked out a piece of blue construction paper. On the top I drew six cats faces — five little ones and one big one.

In the center, I drew a heart. Inside it, I wrote with magic marker:

READ ALL ABOUT IT!
GROWLY, THE CAT,
HAS FIVE NEW KITTENS!

BORN: SATURDAY NIGHT WHILE WE WERE SLEEPING.
WEIGHT: REALLY LITTLE. BUT WE CAN NOT WEIGH THEM BECAUSE WE ARE NOT ALLOWED TO TOUCH THEM YET.

I spent the rest of the morning writing birth announcements. When I finished I

was going to deliver them to my family and friends.

It was a lot of work. But it was worth it. Babies are special. All kinds of babies. The world needed to know that Growly's had arrived.

Babies

Two weeks later, Andrew and I were back at the big house. Of course, I had called Kristy almost every night to find out how the kittens were doing.

When we arrived on Friday, everyone came to greet us, as usual.

"Hi, everybody! Hi, hi, hi!" I cried. Then I ran to the toolshed to see the kittens. They were gigundoly cute.

On Saturday morning, I waited in the front yard for Hannie and Melody. I could see them both leaving their houses at the same time.

"Hi, Karen!" called Hannie.

"Hi," said Melody. "Could we see the kittens?"

"Sure!" I replied. I felt like I was the proud mother.

"Ooh, look at them!" cried Hannie, when we reached the shed.

"They are adorable!" said Melody.

They really were. They looked more like the TV kittens now. Their legs were still very wobbly. But at least their eyes were open.

"You should have seen them the day they were born. They were sweet, but kind of a mess," I said. "They could not even see because their eyes were closed. Kristy told me they opened their eyes for the first time Thursday morning."

"Can we pet them?" asked Hannie.

I nodded. "Daddy says it is okay to pet them now. We just have to be very careful when we pick them up."

"I will be careful," said Melody.

Gently she picked up one of the gray kittens. Hannie picked up the black one. I petted the other three so they would not feel left out.

Growly was watching us, but she did not seem to mind. I think she knew we were being careful.

"I know what we should play," said Melody, when she put her kitten down. "Let's play house and pretend the kittens are our babies."

"We will need some things from my room," I said. "Follow me."

We went upstairs, then raced back to the toolshed. We brought combs and doll clothes and a little cradle that rocked.

"My, my," said Hannie. "Having quintuplets is hard work."

"Yes, but look at our five lovely children," I said. I gently combed one of the tiger kittens.

"I wonder how this bonnet will look on her," said Melody. She tied the bonnet on

38

the black kitten's head. It was a tiny pink doll bonnet. The kitten did not seem to mind it one bit.

"Put her in the cradle!" I said.

Melody carefully placed the kitten in the cradle. But as soon as she began to rock it, Growly got upset.

"A-rowwwl," she warned.

We took the kitten back out and put her with her brothers and sisters. They were all starting to look a little sleepy.

"It is time for our babies to take a nap," I said.

We agreed on a lullaby to sing them. It went like this:

Night, night, sleep tight,
We'll see you when the sun shines bright.

Our babies were soon asleep. Hannie, Melody, and I tiptoed quietly out of the shed.

Names

"Please, please, puh-lease!" I begged. "Can't I keep one of the kittens? Just one?"

Hannie and Melody had gone home. When I told them that Daddy and Elizabeth said I could not have a kitten, they said I should try one more time. I decided they were right.

But Daddy said, "I am sorry, Karen. The answer is still no."

"We have more than enough people and pets at this house," said Elizabeth.

"I know," I said. "Ten people, counting Andrew and me, and four pets."

"That's right, honey," said Daddy. "Don't you think that is enough for now?"

"I guess," I replied. "But, hey! At the little house there are only four people, counting me and Andrew, and three pets. Can I call Mommy?"

"All right," said Daddy. "See what Mommy says."

I picked up the phone and dialed Mommy's number.

"Hi, Mommy!" I said. "You know Growly and her kittens? Well, they will be needing homes soon. Can I have a kitten of my very own at the little house?" I asked.

Mommy said I could not have one. She thought that three pets were plenty for the little house.

I must have looked very gloomy when I hung up the phone, because Elizabeth said, "I am sorry you cannot have a kitten. But there is something important you can do for all of them. You can find them homes. They cannot leave Growly for at least four more weeks, but after that they will need good homes and people who will love them."

Elizabeth was right. Even if I could not have one of the kittens myself, I still wanted to take good care of them. That was an important job. And if I was going to do it well, I had to get started right away.

"I'll do it!" I said to Daddy and Elizabeth. "I will find those kittens the best homes in the state of Connecticut."

I needed a plan of action. I went upstairs to think. The first thing I decided was that I could not just call them "the kittens." That was not special enough. They needed names. I ran back downstairs and out to the toolshed to study them.

I could not tell which were boys and which were girls. I decided to guess. If their owners needed to, they could change the names later.

The black kitten was awfully slow. In fact, he was pokey.

"That will be your name," I said. "Pokey."

Next came the gray kitten with white on the tip of his tail. That was easy.

"Your name is Tippy," I said.

Then came the gray kitten with the two white paws. She was always bouncing around. I decided she needed a happy name. Like Rosie.

"Hi, Rosie," I said.

I needed two more names. One for the tiger-striped cat with the black diamond on her forehead. I thought about calling her diamond. But that did not sound right to me. I needed another jewel.

"I know! I will call you Ruby," I told her.

I thought the name Bob sounded good with Ruby, so that is what I named the other tiger-striped cat.

There. Five cats. Five names. It was time to take attendance.

"When I call your name raise your paw," I said. "Pokey! Tippy! Rosie! Ruby! Bob! You are all here. Very good," I said.

The first part of my job was done.

Free Kittens!

"Happy birthday, dear kittens!" I sang. "Happy birthday to you!"

It was a big-house Saturday. The kittens were eight weeks old. And boy were they cute!

They were bigger, fatter, and fluffier than before. And they played practically every minute. They were definitely as cute as the kittens on TV commercials.

"Remember to keep the shed closed when we are not around, Karen. I had the doors fixed so Growly and her kittens cannot wander off," said Daddy.

"I will remember," I replied.

Even if Daddy did not want a kitten, he sure did worry about them a lot.

"Now that the kittens are eight weeks old, they are ready to leave their mother," said Elizabeth.

"I know," I said. "I am going to find good homes for every one of them. I am going to start right now."

I went to my room to make a sign. First I drew a picture of the five kittens. Then I wrote in big red letters:

FREE KITTENS!
(YES, THEY ARE REALLY AND TRULY FREE!)

I took my sign and a roll of tape downstairs. Lucky for me, Charlie was in the kitchen.

"Charlie, would you help me? I need to take a chair and a table outside. I have an important job to do," I said.

"I can see," said Charlie, studying my sign. "That looks great. I'll bring out the old card table. You can carry the chair."

"Thanks," I said.

Charlie set up the table. I taped my sign to the front. Then I went to the shed to get the kittens.

A big cardboard box was in the shed. I piled Pokey, Tippy, Rosie, Ruby, and Bob inside. Growly did not look too happy.

"I'm sorry," I said. "But I promise to find good homes for them."

I walked very, very carefully back to the table. I did not want to trip like I had done with the food and water.

"We made it!" I said when I reached

FREE KiTTENs

the table. I set the carton of kittens on it. I kissed each one in case I did not get a chance to say good-bye later.

Then I sat back and waited. And waited. And waited.

Where is Rosie?

"Oooh! This one is so cute!" said Maria Kilbourne. (Maria is eight. She lives next door to Melody.)

"Lookit! Lookit what this one can do!" said Linny Papadakis. (Linny is Hannie's older brother. He is eight, too.)

A big crowd of kids was standing around the front yard. They had all come to see the kittens. I felt gigundoly important.

"Do you think we could take this one home?" said Maria. She was holding Pokey up to her big sister, Shannon.

"He is awfully sweet," said Shannon. "But you know Daddy is allergic to cats."

"Look at that gray one! He just did a somersault!" said Melody's brother, Bill.

"That one is Tippy," I said. "Does anyone want to take Tippy home?"

"I would, but my mommy won't let me," said a girl I had never seen before. "Mommy says litter boxes are smelly."

Claudia Kishi, Kristy's friend, was holding Ruby and petting her. "You are precious," she said. "And look, you have a diamond on your forehead. That makes you very special."

"Hey, be careful!" I called to the boy who was holding Bob. "I don't think he likes being up so high."

Everyone loved the kittens. But no one wanted to take one home. I knew Hannie could not take one because she already had Pat the Cat. And her mommy and daddy would not let her have another. Melody said her family used to have a cat, but it was really old and died the year before. She was not sure if her parents wanted another yet.

"Doesn't anyone want to take a kitten home?" I asked. No one answered.

"Can we put these two on the ground?" asked Linny. "We want to see them race."

"No way!" I said. "They could run away."

I was starting to get nervous. All the kittens were out of the box. I was having trouble keeping track of them. I decided it was time to put them back.

"Okay, everyone!" I called. "The kittens have to go back in the box now. I hear their mother calling them."

Everyone started handing me kittens. I put Pokey back in the box. Then Ruby. Then Bob. Then Tippy.

I counted the kittens. Four. There were supposed to be five. Where was Rosie?

"Who still has a kitten?" I asked. "I am supposed to have one more kitten."

The kids looked at each other.

"I put mine back," said a girl.

"Me, too," said another.

"Somebody must have a kitten!" I cried. But no one did. I felt scared.

"Everyone has to go home now," I called. "Except for Hannie and Melody."

When just the three of us were left, I said, "Come on! We have to find Rosie!"

Karen's Search

"You start looking for Rosie. I will take the other kittens back to Growly," I said to Hannie and Melody.

When I reached the shed, I placed the kittens next to Growly. I made sure the windows were open a crack, so they would have some fresh air. And I made sure the doors were shut tight when I left.

"Sorry about Rosie!" I called to Growly as I raced toward the front yard. "I will not come back until I have found her. That is a promise."

I found Melody and Hannie searching under the bushes. They were calling, "Ro-zeee! Ro-zeee!"

"Any clues?" I asked.

"Nothing yet," said Hannie. "But don't worry, we will find her."

While they searched the bushes, I looked up in our tree. I remembered how on my worst day ever, Boo-Boo got stuck up there. I climbed up to get him even though I had a broken wrist.

If I did not find Rosie, then *this* would be the worst day of my life.

I decided to check the mailbox. Maybe she got in there somehow. But it was empty.

"Ro-zee! Ro-zee!" I heard Hannie calling down the street.

She could be anywhere by now, I thought. Maybe a wild animal got her. A raccoon! Maybe she tried to cross the street and did not look both ways! What if I never saw Rosie again?

Then I remembered something. The lid

was off the garbage can in the backyard. Maybe Rosie jumped in and could not get out.

I looked inside the garbage can. But it was empty.

I decided to check on the four other kittens. I peeked in the window of the shed. Pokey, Tippy, Ruby, and Bob were curled up against Growly. I wondered if they missed Rosie. I sure did.

Suddenly Hannie was standing next to me. She was out of breath. "I . . . ran . . . all the way . . . down the street, Karen. But I couldn't find her."

"And I looked under all the cars on the street," said Melody. "Where should we look next?"

I glanced around the yard. Everything was still as could be. Until the lilac bush moved.

"Look! Over there! In the garden," I said.

Hannie and Melody looked. Everything was still again. But not for long. Two sec-

onds later, Rosie popped out! She jumped in the air trying to catch a fly.

"Ro-zeeeee!" we all shouted together.

I scooped Rosie up in my arms.

"Oh, Rosie, we thought you were gone forever!" cried Melody.

"We missed you so much!" said Hannie.

"Don't you ever do that again," I scolded.

I do not think Rosie knew what was going on. But I bet she could tell we were happy to see her.

I took Rosie straight back to Growly. I was not going to take those kittens out ever again. There had to be a better way to find homes for them. It was time for a new plan.

A Home For Ruby

"Look what I've got!" I said, racing into my classroom Monday morning. Ms. Colman was not there yet, but lots of kids were.

I waved five pictures in the air. They were pictures I took of the kittens at the big house. I was putting my new home-finding plan into action.

I did not want to take the kittens out where they might run off or get lost. And I knew that people needed to see what the kittens looked like. So yesterday, before

Mommy came to pick up Andrew and me, I borrowed Daddy's camera and took the pictures.

"Smile, Tippy," I had said. I wrote Tippy's name on the back of the picture. I took two pictures of each kitten and picked the best ones to bring to school.

Now everyone was crowding around me to see them.

"You will all get a turn," I said, just the way Ms. Colman did.

"Oooh! They are so cute! Especially the little black one," said Nancy. I had told her about the kittens, but she had not seen them yet.

Even Pamela Harding — my sometimes enemy — was impressed.

"All right," I said, "who wants a kitten?"

"I do," said Ricky Torres.

Oh good, I thought. If Ricky Torres takes a kitten, it will be mine too — well, sort of. That is because Ricky is my pretend husband.

"Which kitten do you want?" I asked.

"I would like them all," said Ricky. "But my parents won't let me have a pet."

"Then why did you say you wanted one?" I asked.

"Because I do want one. I just cannot have one," said Ricky.

Bobby Gianelli, Ricky's best friend, thought Ricky was being funny. I thought Ricky was being dumb.

"Okay, then, who can *have* a kitten?" I asked. (I was not going to make the same mistake twice.)

All of a sudden everyone was quiet.

"I guess we have to ask our parents first," said Jannie Gilbert.

"I can have a kitten!" said Natalie Springer. She had just walked into the room and was studying the pictures. "I want *that* one."

Natalie pointed to the picture of Ruby. But then Ms. Colman entered the room.

"Good morning, class. Please take your seats now," she said.

Ricky, Natalie, and I sit in the front row. That is because we wear glasses. We can see better up front. I used to sit at the back with Hannie and Nancy. That was fun. But it was a good thing I was up front today. Natalie and I had to make a plan.

"I will bring Ruby over to your house tomorrow at five-thirty, okay?" I whispered.

"Okay," said Natalie. "I can't wait."

The bell rang and Ms. Colman clapped her hands.

"It is time for attendance," she announced.

I sat up tall. What a great morning! I had already found a home for a kitten. One down, four to go.

Good-bye, Ruby

I hung up the phone at the little house.

"Charlie says he will drive me, Mommy!" I said. "He will take me and Ruby to Natalie's house, then bring me back here."

"All right," said Mommy. "I will drive you to Daddy's now."

Hurray! I was going to the big house on a school day. I was going on an important mission.

When I got there, Kristy and *everyone* were super glad to see me.

"I would like to visit," I said to them,

"but I have work to do. I have found a home for Ruby."

"Yes, we know," said Kristy. "You are doing a very good job."

"Thanks!" I said.

I ran out to the toolshed. I felt happy when I saw Growly and the kittens. But I felt a little sad, too. Saying good-bye to Ruby was not going to be easy.

"You are going to leave your mommy now, Ruby," I said. "And your brothers and sisters, too. But don't worry. I found you a good home with Natalie Springer."

I picked Ruby up and took her over to Growly.

"Say good-bye to your mommy," I said. "And say good-bye to Tippy and Pokey and Rosie and Bob."

When Ruby finished saying good-bye, I carried her over to the box I had brought from Mommy's house. I had put a soft towel and three cat toys in it. I brought a bag of kitten chow, and a bag of cat litter, too.

"Are you ready, Karen?" called Charlie. "It is almost five-thirty. We have to go."

"Ready, Ruby?" I said. Ruby looked as ready as she would ever be. I carried her out to Charlie. He was already in the Junk Bucket (that is the name of his car) with the motor running.

Usually I had to sit in the back. But this time I got to ride up front with Charlie.

"Buckle up," said Charlie.

Before I buckled up, I put Ruby's box and the bags on the floor in front of me. I thought they would be safe there.

Charlie pulled out of the driveway. We were on our way to Natalie's house.

"Did you say good-bye to Ruby yet?" I asked.

"Um, no, I didn't," said Charlie.

"Don't you want to?" I asked.

"Sure. But I thought I could wait till we got to your friend's house," he said.

"You may not have a chance, then. You had better say your good-byes now," I said.

"Good-bye, Ruby. It's been great knowing you," said Charlie.

I thought that was pretty nice. It was my turn.

"Okay, Ruby. You are starting a new life. You will be on your own. Remember everything your mommy taught you. Think of your brothers and sisters often. And be really nice to Natalie. She is going to be your mommy now," I said.

The next thing I knew, Charlie was slowing down the car and pulling into Natalie's driveway.

Oh, boy. Giving a kitten away was hard. Was I really going to have to do it four more times? I hoped it would get easier.

"Good-bye, Ruby. I might never see you again. Good-bye forever," I said.

Welcome Back, Ruby

Sniff. Sniff. I was standing on Natalie Springer's front steps trying not to cry. Charlie was ringing the bell.

For a minute I thought no one was home. Then I heard footsteps and the door opened.

"Hi, Karen!" said Natalie. "Is that Ruby? Oh, she is so cute! Are you sure she is a she? Can I change her name even if she is a she? I like the name Ruby. I do, I really do, but . . ."

"Who's there, Natalie?" called Mrs. Springer.

"It's Karen Brewer, Mommy," said Natalie.

"Hello, Karen. Oh, I see you have brought your kitten. It looks very sweet," said Mrs. Springer.

"Well, she is not really my kitten," I said. "My parents will not let me have one. She is Natalie's kitten now."

I was about to hand Ruby's box to Natalie. But Mrs. Springer had a funny look on her face.

"Natalie? Please explain," she said. She did not sound too happy.

"You *said* I could get a pet, Mommy," wailed Natalie. "And Karen brought these pictures of kittens to school and I fell in love with Ruby and you *said* I could get a pet!"

Uh-oh, I thought. Somebody got things mixed up.

"Yes, I did say you could get a pet, Natalie. But I meant something small and easy to care for, like a turtle or a guinea pig. Not a cat or a dog," said Mrs. Springer. "You should have talked to me first."

"Oh, Mommy, please!" said Natalie. "Please let me keep her."

"I am sorry, Natalie. And I am sorry, Karen. But we are not going to keep the kitten," said Mrs. Springer.

"I understand, Mrs. Springer," I said. "My mommy and daddy said no, too."

Sniff, sniff. This time it was Natalie who was trying not to cry. But she was not doing a very good job. Two big tears plopped down her cheeks.

"I'm sorry you can't keep Ruby," I said. "Maybe someone we like will take her. Then we can visit her sometimes."

Sniff, sniff. "Thanks for bringing her over, Karen," said Natalie.

I thought she was being very brave.

"Good-bye, Mrs. Springer. Good-bye, Natalie," said Charlie.

I carried Ruby's box back to the car. I put the box on the floor and buckled my seat belt. Charlie pulled out of Natalie's drive-way.

I thought I should be feeling kind of bad. After all, Natalie was disappointed. And Ruby did not have a new home. But I did not feel bad. Not one bit. In fact, I felt happy! I bent down close to the box.

"Welcome back, Ruby," I whispered.

Karen's Kitten Party

"**W**e're home! All three of us!" I called when we returned to the big house.

Charlie was being really nice. He agreed to let me take Ruby back to Daddy's house and then drive me over to Mommy's.

"What happened, Karen? Did Natalie change her mind?" asked Elizabeth.

"Nope. Her mommy said she could have a pet. Only she could not have a kitten," I explained. "It was too, too sad."

"What are you going to do now?" asked

Kristy. "You are back to five kittens who need homes."

"Maybe I should take the kittens to the office," said Daddy. "I bet they would be gone by the end of the day."

"No, Daddy! Please don't do that!" I said. "Finding homes for Growly's kittens is *my* job."

"Okay," said Daddy. "I promise you I will not bring them to the office without talking to you first. Now it's getting late, Karen. And tomorrow is a school day."

Charlie drove me back to Mommy's. I had been so happy to have Ruby back. But maybe it was not such a good thing after all.

I could hardly think of anything but the kittens for the rest of the week. I had to find homes for them. And I had to do it myself. It was my important job.

On Saturday (it was a little-house weekend), I called Daddy.

"Hi, honey," he said. "The kittens are all

safe and sound here. Have you found homes for any of them yet?"

"Not yet," I replied. "But I have a new plan."

"The kittens are growing up, Karen. We cannot keep them here forever," said Daddy.

"I just need one more week, Daddy. I promise I will find a home for every one of them by next Saturday," I said. "If I don't, then you and Elizabeth can have my job."

"That sounds fair," said Daddy. "I will see you and Andrew on Friday."

All right! I had one more week to try out my latest home-finding plan. It was a good one. I went up to my room to tell Goosie about it.

"Remember when we had a blue couch and Mommy and Seth wanted to sell it and get a green one? Remember what they did, Goosie?" I said. I could see Goosie did not remember.

"Well, I will tell you what they did. They invited all the people who wanted to buy a couch to come and see it. And you know what? They sold it in one day! So here is what I am going to do, Goosie. I am going to have a kitten party next Saturday. It will be at the big house. (Sorry you will not be there, Goosie.) And it will be inside so the kittens cannot get lost. I will invite lots of kids to come see the kittens. But here is the best part. Only kids whose parents say they can *have* a kitten are invited. And their parents have to come, too," I said.

I was very proud of my idea. I made Goosie clap his paws.

"Thank you, thank you," I said. I took a bow. Then I wrote out my first invitation. Here is what it said:

MEOW!
WILL YOUR PARENTS LET YOU HAVE A
KITTEN?
YES?
THEN YOU AND YOUR PARENTS ARE
INVITED TO A KITTEN PARTY!

I wrote the address of the big house and the time — noon next Saturday. I wrote out lots and lots of invitations. I was going to invite everyone I could think of to my kitten party!

Surprise!

Pop! There goes a red one. I was so excited. I burst every other balloon I tried to blow up. Once I started blowing, I could not stop.

It was Saturday morning at the big house. My party was just two hours away.

"I will help you hang the streamers," said Kristy.

"Thanks," I replied.

Nannie and Elizabeth got the snacks ready — popcorn, pretzels, raisins, and carrot sticks. I put the bowls all around the living room. Then I set out napkins, and paper cups for juice and soda.

There was one job I wanted to do by myself. I wanted to get the kittens ready.

I carried a box out to the toolshed. Growly was awfully quiet. She must have known this was a big day for her kittens.

"Good morning, Pokey, Tippy, Rosie, Ruby, and Bob. A lot of people are coming to see you. I want you to look extra nice," I explained.

I carefully brushed each kitten's coat. I would have washed their faces for them, but they had already done that themselves.

When I finished brushing the last kitten, I put them in the box. I carefully carried it into the house. The clock said ten minutes to twelve. It seemed like ten hours before the doorbell rang. But once it started ringing, it hardly stopped. My kitten party was off to a great start.

"Oh, my! One kitten is just cuter than the next," said Terri and Tammy's mommy.

Terri and Tammy are twins who are in my class. I hoped they would take *two* kittens.

"And this is Ruby. And this is Tippy. And this is Bob," I heard Melody saying. I was glad to see Melody's family. Her parents had decided they would get a kitten after all — if they saw one they really liked.

The phone was ringing in the other room. The next thing I knew, Daddy was calling me. "It's for you, Karen," he said. "It's Mrs. Dawes."

I picked up the phone. "Hi!" I said.

Nancy's mommy had read my invitation. She said that Nancy had never had a pet and she wanted to surprise her with a kitten.

"Nancy has been talking quite a bit about a kitten named Pokey. Is Pokey still available?" asked Mrs. Dawes.

"Yes," I replied.

"Good," said Mrs. Dawes. "Will you hold him for Nancy? Her father and I will give her the kitten as a surprise."

"I sure will!" I said. "I can bring Pokey over tomorrow afternoon when Mommy drives me home."

"Perfect," said Mrs. Dawes.

I returned to the living room. Now only four kittens needed homes. But so many people were at the party. I hoped there would be enough kittens to go around.

Well, some people decided they did not want a kitten after all. But Melody's family was taking Bob. And three more families, besides the Dawes, were taking kittens.

Wow! I did it! I found five homes for five kittens. You can relax, Growly, I thought. They are very good homes. I promise.

Bob

That afternoon Hannie and I went to Melody's house. We wanted to see how Bob was doing with his new family.

"Hi!" said Melody. She was holding Bob in her arms. Bob looked very happy. "Come, on. We can go up to the playroom."

We ran upstairs. We closed the door. Bob jumped into a basket with a quilt inside.

"That is Bob's bed," said Melody. "We

went to the pet store and got lots of things for him."

Melody showed us Bob's litter box, a big basket of toys, a scratching post, and two bowls for food and water. On the bowls were the words, "Here, Kitty."

I picked up a ball with a bell inside. I rolled it across the floor. Bob ran after the ball. He played with it for a while, then stopped.

"Look what he is doing now! He is trying to catch his tail," said Hannie.

Round and round he went. Bob was fast. But his tail was always just out of reach.

"We are going to take him to the vet for a check-up on Monday," said Melody.

"Let's practice taking him now. That way he will not be scared," I said. "Can I be the doctor?"

Melody and Hannie said yes. We made a doctor's office out of two tables and some chairs.

Melody picked up Bob and stepped up to one of the tables. "Hello," she said to

Hannie. (Hannie was the office secretary.) "I have a two o'clock appointment for my kitten, Bob."

"You're right on time," said Hannie. "The doctor will see you now."

"Oooh! What an adorable kitten," I said.

"Thank you," Melody replied.

I looked at Bob's ears. "Clean and pink," I said.

He yawned, and I checked his teeth. "Very white and pointy," I said.

I petted Bob's fur. "Nice and soft."

Melody put Bob down. He started running all around our "office."

"Watch out for the big bulldog in the waiting room!" I called.

"I've got him," said Hannie. She scooped Bob up before the bull dog could frighten him.

We heard a knock on the door. It was Melody's mommy. "Hannie, your mother just called. She would like you to come home now."

"I guess I better go, too," I said. But I

did not want to leave. I did not want to leave so badly that I started to cry.

"What's the matter, Karen?" asked Hannie.

"I do not want to leave Bob. And tomorrow I am going to have to leave Pokey with Nancy. And then I will not have any kittens at all," I sobbed.

"Bob can be your cat, too, Karen," said Melody. "Really."

"That is right," said Melody's mommy. "Bob will live here. But whenever you are at your dad's house, you can visit him."

That was not the same as having a kitten of my own. But I knew that Melody and her mommy were trying to be nice. And I really would visit Bob.

"Thank you," I said.

Then Hannie and I went home. I felt pretty bad. But I knew I would feel better soon. I always do.

Pokey

By Sunday afternoon, I was my old (well, not too old), happy self. How could I help it? I had another important job to do. In a few hours I was going to take Pokey to Nancy's house. What a surprise that would be!

I went into the shed one more time.

"Hi, Growly," I said. "I have come to get Pokey, your last kitten. Guess who is going to take her? My best friend, Nancy Dawes. She lives right next door to Mommy's house."

Growly flicked her furry, gray tail. Growly and I had come a long way since the day I saw her tail disappearing in the doorway. I felt like we were good friends now.

I waited a minute while Pokey said good-bye to his mommy. Then I gently lifted him up. I took him inside the house and carried him to my room.

Pokey, Moosie, and I played together for a while. At first I thought Pokey might try to eat Moosie. But he didn't. They got along very well.

I was reading *Churchkitten Stories* to Pokey and Moosie when Elizabeth poked her head in the door. "Your mommy and Seth will be here soon. Would you like a snack before you go?" she asked.

"No, thanks. I want to get Pokey ready for Nancy," I replied.

I wanted Nancy's first pet to look very beautiful. I brushed Pokey and even tied a blue ribbon around his neck. (I made sure it was not too tight.)

I had just finished tying the bow when I heard the back door slam downstairs.

"Hey, Mom! I went to take Growly her food, but the shed is empty. I did not see her anywhere," called David Michael.

Empty? How could the shed be empty? I had just seen Growly a little while ago. I jumped up and closed the door to my room behind me so Pokey could not get out. Then I raced to the shed to see for myself. If Growly was hiding anywhere, I knew she would come out for me.

I searched every corner of the shed. But David Michael was right. Growly was gone. I ran back inside the house. Everyone was standing around the kitchen. They were all talking about Growly.

"Oh, Daddy, why did she leave?" I asked. "Didn't she like her home here?"

"She is a wild cat, Karen. Wild cats do not have homes. They wander from place to place. She only stopped here to have her kittens," Daddy explained.

"But being wild is dangerous," I said.

"We could have kept her in the shed where she would be safe."

"The only way we could have kept her would have been to lock her inside. And that would not have been fair. A wild cat needs to be free," said Daddy.

I understood what he was saying. But I needed some time to get used to it.

Honk! Honk! Mommy and Seth had arrived. I ran upstairs to get Pokey.

"It is time to go, Pokey," I said. "I am taking you to Nancy's house. You and Nancy are going to get along just fine."

I talked to Pokey the whole way there. I told him that Growly had run off, but that it was okay. And I told him lots of good things about Nancy.

By the time we pulled into the Daweses' driveway, Pokey was ready. So was I. For the last time, I carried a kitten in a box up to the door of his new home.

Part-time Kittens

Nancy's mother was waiting at the door by the time I reached it.

"Hi, Karen. Come on in," she said. Then she turned and called Nancy.

You should have seen Nancy's face when I handed her Pokey's box. I said, "Meet your new kitten! He is a present from your parents."

"Oh, Karen, I can't believe it! Mommy, Daddy, thank you! This is the best surprise of my whole life!" cried Nancy.

Mr. and Mrs. Dawes had smiles a mile

wide. I bet I did, too. I love surprises!

Nancy was holding Pokey up to her cheek. "You are the very one I wanted," she told him.

"I have some things here for Pokey," said Mr. Dawes. "I picked them up yesterday while you and Mommy were at the library."

He brought out a big shopping bag with a red ribbon tied to the handles. It was filled with everything Pokey would need.

"Let's take Pokey up to my room, Karen," said Nancy. "Oh, I am so excited. Thank you for bringing him. And I love the name Pokey. I would not change it for anything."

I was glad. I liked the name too, even if he was not so pokey anymore.

We closed the door and let Pokey explore. Then we emptied the shopping bag. Pokey walked right inside.

"I read in a book that cats like to explore places like empty bags and holes in the

ground. They were born to be hunters. They think they are going to find a mouse or something inside," I said.

"Wow, that is neat," said Nancy. "Hey, Pokey. Here is a mouse for you to catch." She tossed a fuzzy mouse toy into the bag. Pokey started batting it around. The bag was rocking from side to side. Pokey was going wild in there!

"Now remember, you have to be sure he always has fresh water to drink. And you will have to keep the litter box clean, or it gets stinky. And you should take him to the vet pretty soon. We can have a practice visit, so he will not be scared. And . . ."

"You know what, Karen? I think Pokey should be half yours," said Nancy.

"Really?" I said. Now *I* was surprised.

"Yes, I do. Because we are best friends. And because if it weren't for you, I would not have Pokey at all," said Nancy.

"Thanks!" I replied. I knew sharing

would be fine. Nancy and I share lots of important things. Even my best baby doll, Hyacynthia.

Well, I thought, things have not turned out too badly after all. I do not have a kitten of my *very* own. But I have two part-time kittens, Bob at the big house, and Pokey at the little house. That is just right for a Two-Two, like me. And I know where Rosie, Ruby, and Tippy are. I can call and visit them whenever I feel like it.

One bad thing is that Growly is missing. But maybe she will turn up again one day. Maybe she will have another litter of kittens in the toolshed. Growly and I are friends. She can count on me to help her any time.

About the Author

ANN M. MARTIN lives in New York City and loves animals, especially cats. She has two cats of her own, Mouse and Rosie.

Other books by Ann M. Martin that you might enjoy are *Stage Fright*; *Me and Katie (the Pest)*; and the books in *The Baby-sitters Club* series.

Ann likes ice cream and *I Love Lucy*. And she has her own little sister, whose name is Jane.

Little Sister

Don't miss #31

KAREN'S BULLY

"Who is that?" whispered Andrew. (He tried to hide behind Nancy.)

"That is Bully Bobby Gianelli," I told him. Then I yelled again, "What are you *do*ing here, Bobby?"

Bobby smiled. "I am moving to your street. I mean, my family is. We are going to be your neighbors soon. . . . So you better watch out."

I thought of something. "I bet you are not *really* moving to this street, Bobby!" I yelled. "You are just saying that."

"Wrong!" replied Bobby. "We are moving into *that* house." He pointed down the street. He pointed to a house with a For Sale sign in the yard. Pasted over the sign was the word SOLD.

Uh-oh.

LITTLE APPLE®

BABY SITTERS Little Sister™

by Ann M. Martin,
author of The Baby-sitters Club ®

More Titles... ➡

♡ ♡ ♡ ♡ ♡ ♡ ♡ ♡ ♡ ♡ ♡ ♡ ♡ ♡ ♡ ♡ ♡ ♡ ♡ ♡

The Baby-sitters Little Sister titles continued...

❏	MQ47043-4 #44	Karen's Big Weekend	$2.95
❏	MQ47044-2 #45	Karen's Twin	$2.95
❏	MQ47045-0 #46	Karen's Baby-sitter	$2.95
❏	MQ46913-4 #47	Karen's Kite	$2.95
❏	MQ47046-9 #48	Karen's Two Families	$2.95
❏	MQ47047-7 #49	Karen's Stepmother	$2.95
❏	MQ47048-5 #50	Karen's Lucky Penny	$2.95
❏	MQ48229-7 #51	Karen's Big Top	$2.95
❏	MQ48299-8 #52	Karen's Mermaid	$2.95
❏	MQ48300-5 #53	Karen's School Bus	$2.95
❏	MQ48301-3 #54	Karen's Candy	$2.95
❏	MQ48230-0 #55	Karen's Magician	$2.95
❏	MQ48302-1 #56	Karen's Ice Skates	$2.95
❏	MQ48303-X #57	Karen's School Mystery	$2.95
❏	MQ48304-8 #58	Karen's Ski Trip	$2.95
❏	MQ48231-9 #59	Karen's Leprechaun	$2.95
❏	MQ48305-6 #60	Karen's Pony	$2.95
❏	MQ48306-4 #61	Karen's Tattletale	$2.95
❏	MQ48307-2 #62	Karen's New Bike	$2.95
❏	MQ25996-2 #63	Karen's Movie	$2.95
❏	MQ25997-0 #64	Karen's Lemonade Stand	$2.95
❏	MQ25998-9 #65	Karen's Toys	$2.95
❏	MQ26279-3 #66	Karen's Monsters	$2.95
❏	MQ26024-3 #67	Karen's Turkey Day	$2.95
❏	MQ26025-1 #68	Karen's Angel	$2.95
❏	MQ26193-2 #69	Karen's Big Sister	$2.95
❏	MQ26280-7 #70	Karen's Grandad	$2.95
❏	MQ26194-0 #71	Karen's Island Adventure	$2.95
❏	MQ26195-9 #72	Karen's New Puppy	$2.95
❏	MQ55407-7	BSLS Jump Rope Rhymes Pack	$5.99
❏	MQ47677-7	BSLS School Scrapbook	$2.95
❏	MQ43647-3	Karen's Wish Super Special #1	$3.25
❏	MQ44834-X	Karen's Plane Trip Super Special #2	$3.25
❏	MQ44827-7	Karen's Mystery Super Special #3	$3.25
❏	MQ45644-X	Karen, Hannie, and Nancy — The Three Musketeers Super Special #4	$2.95
❏	MQ45649-0	Karen's Baby Super Special #5	$3.50
❏	MQ46911-8	Karen's Campout Super Special #6	$3.25

Available wherever you buy books, or use this order form.

- -

Scholastic Inc., P.O. Box 7502, 2931 E. McCarty Street, Jefferson City, MO 65102

Please send me the books I have checked above. I am enclosing $ _____
(please add $2.00 to cover shipping and handling). Send check or money order – no cash or C.O.Ds please.

Name _____ Birthdate _____

Address _____

City _____ State/Zip _____

Please allow four to six weeks for delivery. Offer good in U.S.A. only. Sorry, mail orders are not available to residents to Canada. Prices subject to change.   BLS995

♡ ♡ ♡ ♡ ♡ ♡ ♡ ♡ ♡ ♡ ♡ ♡ ♡ ♡ ♡ ♡ ♡ ♡ ♡ ♡